Auditing and French Kisses: Whoever Thinks Auditing is Boring Doesn't Know What Happens Between the Numbers.

Martin Muller Audit, Volume 2

Marina Peters

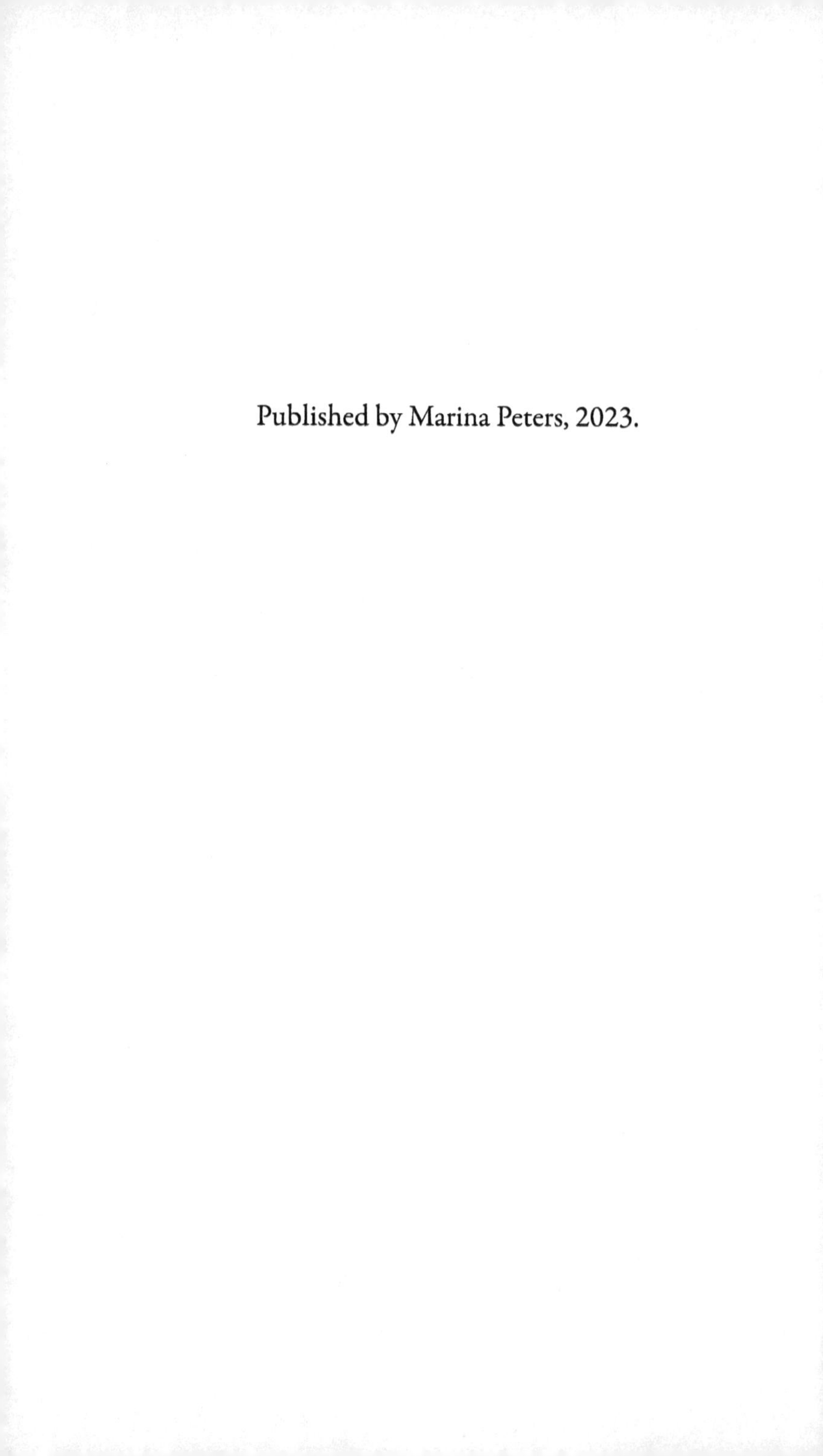

Published by Marina Peters, 2023.

This is a work of fiction. Similarities to real people, places, or events are entirely coincidental.

AUDITING AND FRENCH KISSES: WHOEVER THINKS AUDITING IS BORING DOESN'T KNOW WHAT HAPPENS BETWEEN THE NUMBERS.

First edition. September 27, 2023.

Copyright © 2023 Marina Peters.

ISBN: 979-8223545811

Written by Marina Peters.

Also by Marina Peters

Martin Muller Audit

Auditing and French Kisses: Whoever Thinks Auditing is Boring Doesn't Know What Happens Between the Numbers.

Standalone

How to Generate and Earn Royalty Income

A Steamy Steampunk Cruise

Rare Gemstones and Unknown Precious Stones

Un Caliente Crucero Steampunk

Une Croisière Steampunk Chaude

Generating eBook Income for Intellectuals: A Comprehensive Guide to Creating and Monetizing Digital Books

Watch for more at https://marinapetersbooks.com.

Table of Contents

Marina Peters
Auditing and French Kisses

1

A Martin Muller Audit #2

Auditing and French Kisses

A Steamy Romance Novel

By

Marina Peters

marinapetersbooks.com

"Whoever thinks auditing is boring doesn't know what happens between the numbers."

© Marina Peters

........Chapter I

- Martin –

Luminous Summertime was long gone with the weather pretty accurately depicting my inner spirit. The dark water filled massive clouds that illuminated the sky were perfectly matching with my terribly placid and cold mood. Cold and brisk with a hint of snow. I was miserably sat on my desk, with a sulky face and a throbbing headache from my ultimate hang over of the summer. Thank god for sweet Jen who dropped by to get me a Starbucks and some Advil that helped keep me stable for the day. It was unlike her, after our unfortunate break-up which to be fair was inevitable. She had been keeping her safe distance from me yet lately she has been noticeably frequent in her short visits and small talk.

" Somebody seems to have had a bad day? "

" Bad night. Although, not the entirety of it. Surprisingly."

"Right, not that it's any of my business. I brought some espresso triple shots for you."

" Thank you a ton and ton! I desperately needed these babies."

" I'm sure you do. I'm going to head upstairs. Donny's the new intern who is keen on messing up my systems each step on way."

" Why don't you fire him? "

" Sure. Right, I don't have the authority. " Jen glared at me in what seemed like a pure wrath of disbelief at its finest. She approached forward taking slow steps in her way and placed the hard paper rolled coffee cups on my desk. It was the cardboard roll that labelled " Starbucks " and had my name written on it in all caps.

" Plus, patience is key and he is a pretty good learner "

" Good luck! "

" To you! " She walks out all smug and complacent as good ol' Jen from I.T. always was. Can't believe how good she was in bed. I often take the initiative to please my sexual partners to get it going but she had splendidly impressed me with her hand work. It was painfully tough not to come before she did.

Last night's flashbacks lingered in my mind for hours, it was about time for me to try a threesome, but it blew my god damn mind. It is something I've wanted to try and now that I have it won't be my last time.

A loud pop of brand new Email grabbed my absent – minded intention and who I have been waiting on for ages now. The Email read that I was to be transferred and required in Paris for training. Another check on my bucket list, sex with French women and a fresh cup of Joe at Café Loustic, always heard Heather from op going on and on about it. Heather was a lesbian who in her lists of sexiest women of the world marks French on the top, fascinating how a thought of two women getting intimate created a rush of desire in me and unsolicited thoughts of Jen and Heather.

" You alright there, Martin? "

" Never felt any better, Dick "

'' Just seem a bit weary '' He said dropping his eyes down to the bulge formed in my pants which he had covered with his fists.

'' So you ready to pack your bags? ''

'' I was waiting for a promotion Dick, not passing on my knowledge and wisdom onto other peers who will go off to be on a higher status than my own ''

'' Martin, it is a solid catch for you. Think of it as on – site exposure. If someone had told me to go for a job in a beautiful city as Paris, I would not think twice. Crank it up a notch you are a solid fella! ''

He was a pain in the ass but a pain in the ass who had a valid point. This could be a solid opportunity, rising on the social chain of companies all around the world would be fruitful. Even though I felt slightly discombobulated and how this trip would tire me out. Although, a change of scenario did look extremely appealing. So, with my blurry mind and slippery grounds, I agreed to go to Paris. I sipped on the espresso which shot its pointy daggers precisely at the tough and rough spots of my sloppy mind. It was the kick I need for my day. I began working on my files again trying to cover up the thoughts in my head about Jen and how she knew about my coffee preferences. It is merely an amicable gesture of kindness between two normal friends. Nothing to dig deeper for. Nothing under the lines here. Just friends and nothing more.

........Chapter I I

- Ellis -

My life has been a series of ups and downs, yet the spark that Martin left behind will be my silver lining. Ever since that day, Chris has been religiously focusing on pleasing me in any way the he possibly can, he still hasn't successfully reached on Martin's level yet but he is getting there on a slow pace so I couldn't complain. Martin and I have been texting more frequently than normal with a few calls here and there. He messaged me saying how disturbed he was about having to travel to Paris with Jen after their awkward breakup, they were not even an exclusive couple for long.

" Do you think about that day? " Martin asked me out of the ordinary. We never mentioned it before and now the air was getting thicker and hotter.

" Do I think about what day? "

" The day you lost and found yourself with me inside you "

" Jesus Martin! I don't...ok maybe once in a while I do. I am not afraid to admit it "

" I still do, whenever I need to release myself, you know, lay back and relax. I think about your tight cu- "

" I'll have to stop you right there "

" Don't be such a tight - ass "

" Martin! Do not make me regret giving you my digits. So tell me, when are you leaving? And try to make amends with

Jen over there. You don't' need a grumpy co-worker walking around like a dark cloud of storm and thunder over your workplace. "

'' Talking about digits, mine were pretty worked up in you - "

And I cut him off by hanging up, he got under my skin and that was precisely what had bothered me the most. I need to keep my eyes and thoughts on my boyfriend, but maybe let my mind wander a bit. No shame in reminiscing, I totally lied to him though.

A wild thought had occurred in my mind to visit him and have a one-off, but Chris has been working so hard to keep our relationship exciting. I couldn't and would not do that to him. I wish I was sent to train snotty French women about Auditing and have myself a week away from the village life. Perhaps in the future I can pay him a friendly visit and take Chris along with me.

Or better yet Chris and I could use a vacation time, I turned over my side of the bed and touched his shoulder. Chris was a bed – time reader and he was religiously engrossed in a book called '' Retraining the brain '' by DR. Frank Lawlis.

'' Chris, what do you think about a little vacation? ''

'' Oh wey hey! Where did this come from? ''

'' I'm just suggesting a change of view and relaxation on the sunset beach. Maybe we can go to Paris or Malibu, I could take a few days off of work and you know, you can too ''

'' I'll think about it ''

'' What the hell there that is left to ponder over and about? We can plan it together, get our finances sorted and simply go for it! ''

Chris huffed and sat upright resting his head on the headboard and watched her for a short second.

'' Alright, we will plan something ''

'' Really Chris? Do you think we can afford a little holiday?'' I set on my softest and most effective puppy eyes which works every time like a charm and Chris sighed heave on his spot

'' Don't give me those looks. I think we can make it somewhere in the states. Maybe Hawaii even? We will see ''

I screeched in my side of the bed and launched over his body, grasping his pants' waistband '' Oh fuck! someone's excited! '' he gasped at my action.

'' I love you! ''

'' I love you too, doll. Now come on get over here. It is a cold night and I am feeling a bit exposed and lone 'round here '' Chris wrapped his arms around me and tugged me closer throwing his book across the bed

'' This can be read later. I have an over – worked angel laid all on me that needs to be taken care of''

. . . . .Chapter I I I

\- Jen -

Back at home Jen was slacked on her couch wearing nothing but an orange thong. A half – eaten pepperoni pizza hanging from her lips when she got her email. She quickly texted Martin to check in on him. Even though their previous manoeuvres were a rapid success of professional and personal satisfaction, she wasn't sure taking this path again would be the best thing for her currently. She was a stern person and emotionally detached in their short lived relationship. Jen wanted to be cautious but she knew this trip and experience would open a bag of ugly worms. Even though a trip to France did not in all honesty sound like a terrible idea to her. She immensely loved travelling and all – around exploring different cultures and their people. This could be her chance to gain new memories, get a bit of freely offered exposure to the world.

" Hey, So Dick is sending us on another mission? Paris is freezing this year round "

33

Jen X "

And to her surprise she typed out what her mouth couldn't admit, she missed her pleasant moments with Martin and the holy grail of time she would spend with him was like a cherry on the top.

" It will be fun. Last time I checked you had quite the travel and tourism bug " he texted her back with a cherry emoji and too many Eiffel towers for one text box.

" This isn't a luxurious trip to Toulouse or an Island, it's going to be work to hotel rooms and hotel rooms to airports. "

" Have a leap of faith in me, I'll make it worth your while "

And with the final text I let out a heavy sigh of relief. Martin sounds happy about it and hopefully he won't make our whole and entire week in Paris about him.

- Martin -

The next warm morning, I fled to Paris effective immediately having prepared myself efficiently for both the mundane conferences and Hotel rooms. I texted Jen that it was exciting and I was looking forward to it they were lies. We were both booked at the same La Perrier Hotel and our rooms were adjacent to each other. And so was the entire staff the came from all around the world, this could be a liberatingly fun experience I assume. Always look at the bright side was what my old man always said, something I could not quite get a firm grasp on being a spontaneous soul that I was as a younger man.

Early as a bird, I met her at the airport. She had an over-sized red – berry hoodie on, that was not like Jen at all no skin? Then my eyes trailed lower to notice that she had her pair of ripped and ragged skinny jeans on; that's more like it which I was certain would be thrown off on the plane ride. She looked overly worked up and had bags under her eyes.

" Woke up on the wrong side of your bed? "

She growled aloud and walked past the security check.

" Why am I required here? You are the brains and the teacher there. What on earth would I be doing there? "

" You just need a cup of coffee Jen. Wake those genius senses of yours. "

And she glared at me, I could see her nostrils flaring and decided to remain off her lane for the rest of our way. She certainly was not in a good mood and I didn't need to mess up mine. I was ready for Paris and what it has got in store for me.

<h1>. . . . . .Chapter V</h1>

I was right up at 4:30 A.M in a dimly lit bedroom that smelled like fried chicken and burnt wires. I checked my phone and read an Email from the firm that they had booked our rooms at the Hotel named "La Perrier and guessed it was a fancy haven. So I called Martin right after who was sound asleep judging from the amount of time it took for him to answer the call and his husky voice.

" We leave in two hours chop-chop Tinny "

" Do you ever sleep? "

" Contrary to popular beliefs, I do. Now they've booked our rooms but could you check in with the payment? I certainly can't afford a high profile Hotel in fucking France "

" The expenses are covered, Jen. Don't sweat it "

" Dick never told me why "

" Your impressive technical skills and sweet brains are very much needed there, just as much as my charming presence is. "

".... Meet me tomorrow at 10 "

" Oh Jen, one more deet, your room is right next to mine "

And I hung up with a hum, my thoughts spiralling and memories of our previous rendezvous bring a shiver to my body... my room was right across from Martin's. This time I can't lose my balance again, I have to keep my emotions intact for a torturous period of seven days. Shaking those arousing thoughts I got out of bed to get going to the airport, I can't be late I've got to be strictly punctual.

During the entire flight to Paris, Martin had kept his distance and only asked me two questions, " Did you get your passport? Need a blanket? "

When we took a little holiday together last year everything seemed exquisitely perfect. It seemed like the appealing tranquillity right before a storm wipes out the world beneath your feet and just like that it was over. He was mysteriously obsessed with my private life, interfering in my personal matters and asked me questions I wasn't ready to answer. It's not like we fell in love as we both were two people with contrasting personalities and various different preferences. So we had to end it, even though I enjoyed our little rendezvous and honeymoon phase I had to come to terms with the bitter truth; swallow the pill and shoot the rigid bullet and end it with him. I instantaneously did it, which I assume might have brutally bruised Martin's mountain sized male ego.

Our friendship now is weak, we are not necessarily close friends and never were. We work together so having an awkward environment was not what I practically aimed for, and tried every which was plausible to keep it amiable instead of having a cold war aftermath. If I want this week to run smoothly and successfully I have to set some rules for us; which was to do the job and not the auditor. I have to keep my safe distance from his charming and alluring ways.

And so, through - out our long hours' trip on air I fell asleep with my stretched over the seats. I could occasionally hear Martin's voice as he chattered with shudder – less ease with the air hostesses out of ear shot. He might have visited the toilet twice and then spent the rest of the hours on flight board watching a movie quietly on his head screen. Martin's resemblance to a ten year old child is so comically uncanny. He can be obnoxiously loud and chit – chatty when in the mood for socialising. Yet, he can be a complete opposite and contrasting persona of that bubbly personality when he is focusing on a project on hand or busy with something that managed to grab gold of his interest for longer than 5 minutes.

. . . . .Chapter V I

- Hotel 3 P. M. -

The exclusive hotel lobby was decorated with modern aesthetic art hangings and Greek statues, which Jen gazed wide eyed at. Martin admired her tough exterior and how sensitive she truly was beneath it all, goth and scary with a kitten sized heart full of hearts and sprinkles.

They were escorted with a trolley carrying their luggage, up till the fifteenth floor. Rows and rows of rooms piled and ran ahead of them on each floor and they escalated in the glass golden elevator. It was facing the middle hall of the massive place, it looked like a reputable place located in a fancy area of northern Paris.

Inside their rooms they had a couple of welcome tray which consisted of elegantly arranged flowers, chocolates and 2 tiny bottles of Rose. They had a list of itinerary along with the map of the Hotel, since their conferences will be acutely held and arranged in the Hotel's very own venue.

The conference room was neatly organised in the spacious venue, with orderly aligned large mahogany tables. Significantly, arrayed chairs were allotted across 2 large smart boards. Four large tables were orderly positioned between the desk chairs and the smart boards. Fresh lilac was implanted in metallic gold vases elegantly blooming creating a rich and elegant ambiance in the room.

There was a garden view bar side that rested in the basement section of the Hotel. It displayed an impressive collection of bottles and had a winery corner right across the windows which disclosed a spectacular garden. They even had a golf course within a few meters of the Hotel premises which was splendid compared to a club house quality.

A large biased collection of aligned boards hanged on the wall by the doorway right behind the receptionist's table area. They were elegantly embarked with silver lining calligraphy which named various locations and directions pointing towards the desired destinations: Gym sec, Pool side sec, Golf course sec, Broit Bar sec, Heaven Spa and massage sec etc.

.... **Chapter VII**

- Martin -

It was busy Monday, which starting off with us rushing to the conference room. Different men and women of various sizes and ethnicity, their cheerful chatter filled the room. I introduced myself and they all applauded me, looking awfully way overexcited for an auditing session. So I grabbed my coffee and waited for Jen to connect the monitor as she prepared the projector.

" Could everyone take their seats so we start this session? "

" Dude, aren't you going to wait for Celine? "

" Who the hell is Celine, Jen? "

" Uh... your manager on board? Ring a bell? " she asked looking as dazed and confused as the rest of the crowd in the room. Well this is embarrassing.

" Right. Celine! She's clearly not on the scheduled time so we'll have to start without her "

" Martin technically, the session starts on 8:15 and it's 8' o clock now "

" Thank you, Jen. You can take your seat now. Or leave "

She left the room giving me the most atrocious glares and I couldn't care less. This was my time to shine and a spot on my reputation had no room in room in my aim for today's session. I had also decided to keep my head on the clear shore of professionalism and not mingle with any of these drop dead gorgeous females who were around the count of 11. There were 20 different nationalities and I could easily make my way through the globe right then. I have not seen a level of diversity this far in my entire life, from Indonesia to Netherlands and Germany to New Zealand. But for now, I have a bigger agenda in mind.

Extremely blazed up for my first and foremost session of imparting my great wisdom to a group of peers, I walked straight head into the mud.

"I'm going to dip my feet right into it, and begin by defining the process of Auditing- even though we all could say in it our sleep. It's rudimentary " I say rolling my eyes which gets a few short giggles and I sneer at Jcn who looks properly unimpressed.

So I continue with my lesson, " It's an assessment and ascertaining of financial, operational and strategic goals in firms to determine whether they are in compliance in the stated principals- "

A short click of heels and dash of the door grab my attention, and a lovely brunette walks into the room looking in utter disarray.

" Bonjour! "

A tall and skinny women walk in greeting everybody, she studies me and drops her bag and coat onto the table.

" Starter without me I see "

I shake her hand as she extends her arm towards me, her skin was smooth yet she had a firm grip. Confidence, maybe over – confidence is what I will be dealing with here.

" Time is money. Can't wait for too long Mrs...?"

" Celine Ford "

The French – woman was now sneering at me. Her glitter swiped eye lids rapidly fluttered as she studied my body and then the room.

" Martin Muller, Pleasure to meet ya! "

" Shall we? "

" Yes go ahead "

" So everybody has met and greeted each other I hope. Let us get back to the matter on hand. The base of au- "

" Pardon Mr. Muller ? "

" Martin, you can call me Martin "

" Sure, I hope you do you mind starting fresh again? I wouldn't want to miss any part of the session. Of course, you weren't as consistent with your professionalism act as you were with the time management " she spat her words with a neat and posh accent which sounded easy on her lips yet the words that weren't very polite came out to sound like honey and milk.

" We didn't cover much until you barged in "

" I insist "

The whole room seemed to mix up with palpable emotions of bold fear and sensational suspense. I nodded in response to her request, which seemed more like an or order or challenge. Narrating the entire sentence once more for the bossy French woman in red, I complied even against my own rules. Across the room I could see Jen's smug expression with her raised eyebrows. It was either pure shock or her being impressed with the cockiness.

- Hotel lobby 8 P. M. -

Chatter filled the room of a lavishly organised bar-side, clinks of glass and laughter. The ladies seemed to have taken a well-deserved break, after their first session to have a leisure time to connect with their peers.

" So our trainee is kind of hot, he's got arms of a log "

" Jenna!! Oh you are right though "

" I bet you can have sex without touching the floor with him "

Right then, their trainer, Martin walks into the lobby all eyes on him. He feels his confidence perk up and grows a smug look on his face.

" You aren't nailing these under- construction international auditors, Are you Martin? "

" What? Why would you say that? "

" Considering your disgraceful and vain history of course "

" Just stay in your lane, Jen "

" What is it with you ever since we walked in here you have been nothing but horrible to me "

" Pardon "

They hear a familiar French accent and the similar rich aura from the lady manager, Celine. She walks right past them not giving them a single eye out and Martin's in for the devouringly challenging game.

'' Cold war, you started it. I like her already '' said Jen and Martin glared at her faking a sheepish grin

'' I like a little challenge Jen, rush of the chronic chase ''

'' Have it your way, I'll be here watching. Alert and observant with my popcorn, enjoying the show ''

'' Yea alright, have it your way ''

'' Don't try embarrassing yourself for god's sake, she will eventually come around. It's not like you forgot her name or pay her proper attention, or you know, disregard her totally and completely ''

'' Alright, alright. That's enough out of you. '' Martin grabbed the drink off of Jen's hand and gulped it in one sip

'' Straight vodka? ''

'' Whaaat? I am steaming it off ''

'' Clearly enjoying way too much, we have to up early tomorrow ''

'' You don't have to inspect me. I am here to capably perform my job as you are ''

'' I'll get out of your hair then ''

'' Go ahead, I insist '' she said in an imitative French accent and Martin stormed out of the bar

.... .Chapter X

- Jen –

The morning started off pretty early and the head start was awful. Martin was being a complete asshole to me, but work is work and I need the money. I am pleased though that I would not have to worry about him being inappropriate and sketchy with me. I consistently reminded myself that it's only for 6 more days of hell and heaven, the first being working with Martin co-dependently and the latter being Paris, the city deserved to be viewed and toured, leave no stone unturned.

Heather had given me a well presented list of places which was jotted and lined with plenty of site seeing spots to visit. I took my bag pack to get going and explore France. Throwing my problems and Martin right behind, if you can't make it, bury it. That's what I always say.

I had booked an early morning guided tour of this incredible museum that houses the largest collection of impressionist and post-Impressionist masterpieces in the world. Painters including Monet, Degas, Renoir, Cézanne, Gauguin, and Van Gogh. My passion for sculptures is over – rated and it has always been a passion of mine to get myself enrolled in one of those habitual pottery session classes. I read my tourism booklet which displayed a description of the museum:

The history of the museum, of its building is quite unusual. In the centre of Paris on the banks of the Seine, opposite the Tuileries Gardens, the museum was installed in the former Orsay railway station, built for the Universal Exhibition of 1900. So the building itself could be seen as the first "work of art" in the Musee d'Orsay, which displays collections of art from the period 1848 to 1914.

Open from 9.30am to 6pm daily, except Mondays
Late night on Thursdays until 9.45pm
Last tickets sold at 5pm (9pm Thursdays), museum cleared at 5.30pm (9.15pm Thursdays)

After strolling down the crowded museum I rushed to get some food in my system. All the walking and feet work got me worn out, even though I took a guided tour, remembering Heather's stern tone in my head " If you're visiting the Orsay for the first time, one of the best ways to get an exciting overview of the periods and artists featured at the museum is to take a guided tour. Don't be stupid and while booking a ticket make sure to mention about a request for a tour guide as well. "

The restaurant in the museum was up the stairs and also had an awesome display of colourful glass art. I ordered some penne pasta with pesto sauce along with a side pine nuts and spinach salad. I cherished being present in the moment, surrounded by complete strangers who didn't even speak the same language as me. It was a liberating exposure, as it has always been my dream to visit Paris alone since I was a little girl with tomboy boots and a Barbie skirt. Another thing I was utterly grateful for was that no one from the hotel had interrupted my empiricism. My wonderful experience of solitude was basically mind blowing. So much so, after a while I even questioned my practically eminent decision of going back to the hotel or just walking around the stranded streets of the night life. But my thoughts were intruded by Martin calling to check on my where – abouts,

" So you just headed out without me? "

" Don't such a spoilsport. I wanted the day for myself "

" Alright, whatever. I will be going out tomorrow with the whole team to sightsee around and I was actually calling to ask if you wanted in? "

" Oh, that sounds like fun. The entire team coming along like a work day out – doors."

" So? "

" So yea, I'll join you all. You can definitely count me in. And where are we going by the way? "

" We will all be out at 8 A.M sharp to collectively go on a Cruise along the River Seine. It is supposed to be this magical ride along the river side and the blissful bridge in the ticket agent's precise words "

" Sounds amazing, I will head back now to pack for tomorrow, can we go for a swim too? "

" I don't think so, it's a tourism cruise that lasts for 1 - 2 maximum blissful hours "

" Sounds good. Wait, hold on. Are you not usually sea sick? I vividly remember how you denied the short boat ride back in our trip "

" True, but I everybody voted and picked a place that was chosen by the majority of the group. Which seemed to have defied my suggestion of visiting local museums and libraries. They said it has a low level deck where it felt safer and much environmental friendly. So I' am taking their word for it. "

" Alright, it's nice to see you take up a chance like that. Even though you were such a pussy with me "

" Well, new things happen every day and there is a first time for everything right? "

" Right "

" So well, consider this mine "

" Uhuh, considered. You are still a pussy. "

" I will see you tomorrow. Goodbye, Jen "

" Yea you will. Bye "

Martin had an unforgivable way of affecting me and he always made sure to expertly use that to his full advantage. I would not label my affectionate feelings towards him as " love " but they were pretty constantly visceral and long – lasting. Supposedly we could end up together in the long run, if we had a chance at that. Martin is a hard one to keep, he is like a dessert you can't get enough of. I enjoyed his company as well, just as much as he does. I'm sure it's pretty apparent how well we both fit in together. Some crucial part of the reason why we are more frequently than not, paired together for projects are how well we tend to work together. We fit like jam and butter, Martin was a smooth talked he always had the right thing to say. And I was the tinged flavour needed that would burst your tongue buds. Even though I wasn't sure what I felt for him was love, I had to figure it out sooner or later. I walked down a slim path of chipped stairs on my way out to the street. Stepping into the cab I had ordered I spent the car ride wondering how life had worked its miracle to get Martin and I together for another time round.

.............Chapter X I

- Hotel lobby 8 A. M. -

It was in the early hours of the day and everybody from the Auditing team grouped up in the hotel lobby, awaiting their ride to the cruise – boat. They gathered up outside as the red tourism bus showed up and honked at them. In an automatically allotted sequence the whole group piled up and took their seats at the bus as some squealed with joyous excitement and others groaned over their hang – overs with a complete distaste.

Jen was obviously amongst the middle tier of both these groups. She wasn't necessarily repulsed by the idea of joining over 20 people on a public transport over to the boat ride that was 3 hours long. But her late night shenanigans with some of the team peers last night had her head flimsy and thoughts twisted in a messy piles of nutty knots.

While Martin and Celine were seated night next to each other, the women behind them talked about body cleanse and hygiene.

" I tried the Kambucha method, it didn't seem to have worked it's magic on me " A voice that belonged to a lady in her late 40's c called Jean spoke out diligently

" You should read Jeanne Menal's juice cleanse method, it was a wonderful experience for me. I took her juice mix recipes and they honestly have done wonders. Right under a week I could feel my body cleanse, the diarrhoea is not a side effect but simply and truly effective! "

" Oh really? I will give it try once I land back in Manchester. My daughter Charlotte has her doubts about juice cleanses. I say, don't knock it till you try it "

Martin wrinkled his nose on the choice of topics that were announced behind them, and Celine let out a short snort

" Real talk about emptying your bowels is not what I had in mind, especially on my way to a serene place " Martin laughed as he spoke to Celine.

She looked extra sexy today with her hair tied up in a casual bun, golden highlights complimented her curls that fell upon her bare shoulders. She was someone with a fit body and Martin took a wild guess of her being in a consecutive Yoga and Pilates membership. She had a floral sundress on and tan slippers. Her eyes appeared relaxed and soothing under the morning sun rays.

" I am quite certain at their age you would speak of similar matters and more. They have to care about their health "

" Yea but it's 8 15 A. M. on the clock and on a good, good morning like this! " He swayed with fingers outside the window show – pointing towards the green painted scene and running clouds.

" It is a good day. You were pretty lucky in that aspect. You wouldn't prefer cruising along the river – side under horrific rains and thunder – storms I presume "

" I actually enjoy rain "

" Of course you do, Mr. Muller " Celine muttered under her breath but it was loud enough for Martin to hear.

Captivating panoramic view had the guests on board completely awestruck as they snapped endless amounts of pictures and recorded lines of videos. Melodically sad French music played on deck along with the chitter – chatter of the people. The boat paddled across a magnificent view of a rather tranquilising river. They swept their way under a large bridge with had pedestrians and tourists who were engrossed with photography. In the beginning of the cruise ride a petite man with delicate voice explained and talked about some history of the area which Jen was clearly least interested in.

The weak Tour man's commentary provided a brief historical information and anecdotes about the different buildings, bridges, and neighbourhoods. They were later to have lunch on the open deck area with a adequately presented table. It had classic French breakfast and lunch meals arranged on blue – ish green plates that resembled the ambiance of the river water. Soft squeaks and chirrups of birds could be heard from across the bridge.

Jen made her way zig – zagging through the owling crowd and sat on the bench beside Martin.

" I have to say, this was totally the best decision you have ever made in your life. And I for one am happy to be here "

" Really? Look who has decided to come around! "

" How are you feeling? With your sickness and stuff"

" I am alright. I feel great! Have you tried this pink juice they handed to us when we entered? "

" Yea, it tasted like an overly - liquefied lemonade "

" Celine told me it would help with my sickness and it did. "

" Oh Celine, of course she did "

" What? What is that tone I'm hearing? "

" Nothing at all enjoy your pink French medicine "

Jen took hold of her fork and pinched her almond sprinkled croissants with force.

" Honestly, Jen you need to stop with the jealousy. "

" Excuse me? "

" You and I were a thing back in the days –

" Oh back in the days? When exactly was that? A hundred thousand years ago? "

" What? You are not even making sense right now. "

" What do you want from me Martin? "

" Why do you keep asking that? I thought we were past the strange stage of post- relationship dilemma. We were on good terms "

" Good terms? You never called me back and acted like I did not exist in your world! "

"Listen, I'm going to paint a clear picture for you and set some guidelines straight. We might be still attracted to each other, you are a beautiful woman and incredibly genius per that say. And I'm well " He shrugged his shoulder as if suggesting an obvious fact. " I tend to drive women my way like moth to flame. But you and I just don't work. We don't "

" I am going to stop you right now Casanova. I don't want to hear any of your guidelines or any of that shit " Jen grabbed the flamboyant River Siene Brochure from the table and with a loud jerk of the seat she stood on her feet

" Maybe have some of those apple Martinis and settle that temper of yours huh? " Martin yelled back at her from his propped seat.

As Jen's small figure dissolved in the view of laughing and jumping pupils. Celine's sublime body appeared out of it. She glanced back at Jen who stomped her feet a little too hard on the wood surface and came over to replace her position. Her hair gracefully flew in the European breeze which she had apparently set loose and they rested on her shoulder. She set her plate of the red striped table cloth and gingerly placed a creamy bronze napkin on her lap.

" Girl trouble? "

Martin sipped his double espresso shot with a sniff that awakened his sleeping mind.

" Err not really. We are colleagues and no funny business "

" Not what I have heard "

Celine meticulously grabbed her fork and knife and dug into her neatly sliced sesame bread and swiped some butter on it.

" What have you heard then? Humour me "

" I am not one to invest in the non – sense of unofficial rumours , not exactly a seller of gossip "

" You did ignite my flame of interest by throwing a comment about it "

" Suit yourself " she whispered against the rim of her caramel cappuccino, her

" So you are going to leave me dry and high? "

" If it means I won't dip my hands in impeccable dirt, Yes "

'' Thank you, by the way for recommending that magical potion it seems to have quickly cured my sea – sickness ''

'' You're welcome Mr. Muller ''

'' Martin, please ''

'' Mr. Muller '' she insistently announced my last name while disregarding my request of being addressed by my first name. And I knew in the moment that this gorgeous woman ahead of me was up for a solid chase, then and there.

- Martin -

A week with a snotty Frenchwomen is not what I'm looking forward to. I have ought to get on her good side as quick as plausible.

I went back to my room to find Jen laid back on the couch, a pack of Cheetos scattered on her lap and an open laptop. I needed to get back and relax for another day of stressful audit sessions and unnerving social gatherings in the bar downstairs. I also needed to find a bar that's located anywhere in the distance of 2 meters. Sleeping with colleagues wasn't permissible but no rules were mentioned against picking strangers and having a bit of fun. The little cruise tour had me *tired,* and the last thing on my mind was to hear another mocking comment or pick another fight with Jen.

" Did you check your phone? "

I flipped my phone out my back pocket to read through the texts sent by Dick, of course Dick.

" So he needs us on another project? "

" Are you surprised? "

" Not really, I'm the best he's got "

" Oh, so it's present and perfectly intact " Jen muttered throwing a couple of hot Cheetos into her wide open mouth and wiping her hand on the napkin

" What is? "

" Your confidence is " she said mockingly with her eye brows questioning me

" I assumed it was harshly bruised, you know, by that French woman, Celine " she enunciated the name thickly as she meekly dragged out her pink tongue to fixate on the letter " L "

" Yeah, she's got bit of a bitter attitude towards me, I'm a hoot " I grabbed a cold water bottle out of my fridge and took a long sip

" It's common to despise someone who doesn't respect your professional status "

" Despise? That's a strong word Jen. More or so, coming from you. "

Jen rolled her eyes at me in response and continued to work her fast fingers on the device. She seemed soothed and relaxed, no recollection or residue of our bitter argument from earlier today. That's what I enjoyed about Jen, she was not one to hold a grudge. Her brain worked fiercely at the speed of her limbs and she had no time to let trivial matters holding her back.

" So did you receive the memo? " *Changing the topic, Classic Jen*

" Dick? "

" Yup, Dick "

" He wants me to check the accounts of Schrkel's Company. It is not specifically difficult though. He just wants me to audit a large corporate company in Brisbane. Apparently it is an important client Have you done the background check? "

" I am not your assistant. Figure it out by yourself, you are a smart bean "

" Why are you here again? " I asked her rudely, she was starting to get on my nerves and her constant disregard to personal space during our time here was spewing fuel to my anger

My harsh remarks must've hit the desired spot, because now Jen had a furious glare, red cheeks and she stood up from her relaxed previous position

" I'm here because Dick unmindfully sent me to assist you with the technical support required for your teaching sessions, I'm not here to please your needs or to feed your unsolicited desires. So get your head back in the game before you begin to develop delusional ideas, Martin. Believe it or not, contrary to popular belief, not every woman who breaths next to you within half a meter of distance dreams and jumps at the opportunity of sleeping with you. "

Her eyes were darker in shade and deep melancholy was painted roughly on her expression as she spoke those words of honesty.

And with that claim she launched out of the room grabbing her stuff with her. Good riddance. The last thing I wanted to deal with right now was two angry women. I went to bed sorting and statistically planning ideas to win these two women over, not because I need them by my side but because I'd rather spend my time resourceful time efficiently than have Jen and Celine riding dragons round my head, causing more trouble than I required.

Nonetheless, convincing and coddling Jen is pretty simple. My efficient years' experience of working with her has proper educated me on her personality and behaviour. It's rubbing Celine the right way is what drove me crazy. I needed more information to work with, and she was a tough woman to flatter up. Generally, I'm a sweet-talk induced people person, but Celine seems to be a quite obsequious person who was two steps ahead of me. None of my usually old and sleazy games or ass-licking tricks seemed to have been sufficient or effective with my goal of winning her over.

I flipped my Mac – book open and searched for Celine Chrystal Walter. She was born and raised in North London, explains the latest designer shoes and outfits. She was well put, her style was more high – standard and elegant. Moved back to Paris at the age of 14 and at the age of 16... oh she worked for Play Boy Magazine. There was a link that neatly displayed a colourful grid of her photoshoot images. She was a stunning, just stunning. Standing naked in a confident posture lent against a stair – way railing. Another shot of her on a flower bedsheet barely covering the side of her glorious butts. I got worked up looking at her lavish full breasts and her lady parts had a shadow of what looked like very smooth hair. I slid my hand under the sheets and gripped my hard dick, stroking myself tightly visualising her hot and sweaty body on my bed. Her French accent surprisingly turned me on harder, I heard her sexy voice moaning out my name. My vision turning blurry and sweat dripping down my back.

After successfully jerking off to this gorgeous woman, not once, not twice but four times; I thought of ways I could use to win her over. I decided the only way I could climb a good ladder with her was to convince her to go out with me, share a meal. I wonder how she will react if I told her what I had just done, pretty sure Jen heard me banging on the headboard. Not that it mattered to me what Jen's opinion was about my sexual fantasies or activities.

43

................Chapter X I V

- Celine -

Martin

Martin Muller, he was as turbulent as an over - powered American Jet. His eyes were stern but had a sad story be, hind those drapes of sharp confidence and piercing gaze.

I cautiously studied him under my microscopic eyes, he seemed like an honest man who deceived himself on a daily basis. In order to work with him hand in hand I had to analyse his behaviour and personality. His bubbly demeanour says he is easy going, his quick wit induced tongue says he is intelligent. Yet his unprofessional mannerism suggest he is nothing but a large old prick. I heard out of ear – shot many a times about his playful tricks of getting women in bed, and how Jen was the one who lured men in her illicit direction and there's always two sides to a story. Even though I chose not to believe those harsh rumours there was no denying that what these two possessed was merely a friendly dispute.

Moreover, I had skilfully studied his file previously as I generally do with all of my to – be work partners. What took me by a spur of surprise was that his achievements were quite impressive, yet it does not line up with his level of employment choices. He's clearly an exquisite asset to his company, who can leave as he pleases but there is something poignant holding him back. It could be his interest in that Jen technician girl or any other aspect of his job back home.

What is it Mr. Muller, I strongly wonder what it is that's keeping you out of reach. I watched his stupidly large image presented on the banner advertisement near the conference room. Large smiles with a beautiful set of pearl teeth, starry eyes combined with a strong and meekly hulky physique. He is a good – looking charmer.

" I chose it myself "

I turned around in a haste to spot him standing there across me, same shark teeth sinking into my skin. Irritable was added to the list of his personal traits. I tried to walk away but he stepped ahead of me blocking my way towards the hallway

" It's a beautiful day, what do you say I take you to lunch? "

" We still have 20 minutes ahead of us, come on what do you say? " he added when he didn't get any response from me

" Mr. Martin "

" It's just lunch, look, I know we both started off on the wrong foot but I would love to redo it all "

" Just lunch? "

" Just lunch "

" Is it far? We have only around- "

" 30 minutes left. Yes, don't you worry about it. The place is just round the corner, so we won't take long and make it back in time "

" 29 minutes now "

His smile grew bigger and wider as he guided me out the hallway into the elevator. He smelled so good, added to his list.

" So where is this place we are going at? "

" Let me surprise you "

'' You know I live here, no? ''

He laughed weakly, '' Yes, I do. After you ''

'' So today's topic requires a bit of hands on job, so would you be able to handle 40 people or should we divide 20 – 20? ''

'' Sounds good. Also, what do you say we don't talk about work right now? ''

'' But we are colleagues ''

'' I know, anything else please? It can be anything at all ''

Damn he is very enticingly convincing and polite

. . . . .Chapter X V

- Jen -

My morning started off with Martin barging into my room without knocking. He brought me breakfast while I showered, and apologised for his crude behaviour.

" You know how worked up I can get, Jen. Let's get you cleaned up and set for the day. Look I even got us classic French breakfast "

He held a tray full of miniature croissants of various fillings, and a cheese board consisting of a cheese tower, obviously made my him. Two glasses of black fresh espressos and other two of what looked like pink lemonade with basil seeds.

" That's not a classic French breakfast! You, moron. "

" Wow. I'm concerned for your choice of triggering words. Now can you please get dressed so we can get this food in our system and head for our next session? "

I huffed a loud sigh and headed towards my bathroom grabbing a tiny croissant off the ceramic white plate.

" Do you need some help? Some careful assistance with un – dressing or the act of steamy showers? "

" Fuck off, Martin "

The croissant was delicious, but that wasn't what shifted my grumpy mood. Martin being apologetic and realising his mistake was a new thing I could get used to it.

. . .

During the class Martin was constantly stealing looks and smiling at me, this man is trouble. Or maybe I was in for a trouble either way I had to divert my mind from his sick smile and the urge to kiss him right against that white major smart board he had presented a grid of numbers and solutions on.

" Risk assessment is the identification and analysis of relevant risks to the achievement of an organization's objectives, for the purpose of determining how those risks should be managed.

During the risk assessment process, Internal Auditing identifies and assesses both the likelihood and potential impact of various risks to the organization. " he gave me another glance my way and looked away to continue with his gibberish

" Internal controls are then identified and evaluated to determine how adequate they are in reducing risk to ensure that residual risk is at manageable levels. Residual risk is the risk that something will occur after controls or procedures are implemented to prevent it. In addition to audits required by state regulations, those activities or functions with higher levels of residual risk are typically selected for audits. "

I started studying the students, the assistants. Some of them seemed lost in their own mind, while their eyes sharply set on their Mentor, their mind was in an alternative state. I heard my name being called and went towards Martin.

" Now here you will see I've allotted some risks involved numbers of companies on line, and you are required to – oh. Jen? Need you here Jen! "

" Coming "

I rushed towards him like in quick steps

" Can you fix this screen seems to be stuck and the wires were plugged in just right "

" Sure "

While fixing the problem on hand I glanced towards a woman in red pantsuit, eyes burning Martin's physique. She was delicately biting her lip and circling her fingers over the round of her knees. When I looked over at Martin, who was watching her back I noticed him being uncomfortable for a mere second before he took his eyes off of her.

" Here you go, it works just fine now. You can go ahead with your session. Excuse me "

I excused myself and walked out of the room in a gist, hearing Martin's steep voice

" The WIU Office of Internal Auditing develops the annual audit plan using a risk-based approach. The annual risk assessment process occurs in late spring or early summer to facilitate the development of a two-year audit plan. Internal Auditing conducts the risk assessment process through discussions with management; review and analysis of budgets and proposed programs; and a systematic evaluation of risk factors covering the- "

I rushed back into my room to wash my face with cold water, it was hard being a jealous kind. I heard a bing on my phone and got alert. When I went to check what it was I felt my heart race again, it was Martin

" Meet me in my room, Yellow suits you. XXX "

Vivid images of our past struck out again, I couldn't help but think of what could he possibly want from me. Wasn't he checking out chic women like Celine and Marta? I was just a sexual rebound for men like Martin. I still wanted him even if made me feel like a desperate mad piece of fuck. I tugged on the loose thread on my cashmere sweater, pondering over ways to lure Martin in my direction. I wanted him to want me, in better words I wanted to fuel his explicitly virile nature. I thought of all the fixable techniques that would work in this current situation being in a bit of a pickle myself. Perhaps dressing provocatively would help me gain his attention, or ignoring him out of the picture would work wonders.

. . . . .Chapter X V I

- Martin –

My room was my safe haven and I decided to never let any work weigh me down. In order to fully enjoy my time here I had to get the dust off my desk and finish the extra work Dick had emailed me about. I grabbed my phone and dialled the digits that were written in the informative email under contact information.

'' Hello, I'm Martin Muller from (company's name) organisation and I'm calling to make a quick audit of your company. ''

'' Hello Martin, you are talking to the right person then. I am Josh Simpson, the supervisor of the Scherkl Corporate ''

'' I apologise for not being personally present. I'm currently located in Paris or It'd be a pleasure to visit Brisbane and perform it in person. ''

'' Oh that's alright! Mr. Gallenger would have appreciated your presence but it's completely understandable that you were in a compromising position already ''

'' Thank you, you are a nice person! How are you doing, Mr. Simpson? ''

'' I'm doing well. Thank you! How are you doing Martin? Ready for the job? ''

'' I'm fine. Hahaha Yes, I am ready ''

'' Take the wheel mate ''

" Well to begin with, can you please provide me with the details of all sums of money received and spent by the company? "

" Yes, sure I can. Would you like it on email or right now vocally?

" Vocally please "

" Alright here goes, better grab a pen mate. The money received and spent is as follows:

Total money received = 100m

Total expenditure = 75m

" Um. Will you please send me a detailed report to my email address? "

" Sure thing, you will receive it by end of the day without fail. "

" I would like to have few pieces of info on your HR department. Does your company provide and maintain other special programmes for treating employees? For example:

Employee recruitment and selection

Training and coaching

Performance evaluations

Wages, working hours, and employment conditions. That sort of thing "

" Well, we have a dedicated team for recruitment. Once we recruit people, we train them for a month from their joining dates. Their performance is evaluated every six months. The employees are paid on 3rd of every month. Our company timings are from 9 A.M. to 6 P.M. "

" Coming to the finance department, does the company use an accounting software system that provides a full range of functionality? If yes, do people working in the account department understand how to best use the system? "

" Yes, our finance department does make use of software named Quicken Premier from Intuit. This accounting software helps in budgeting, investing, reporting etc. Our employees in finance department are well trained to use this software "

" Very well. We are left with the last part of the audit. Has the company created and does it maintain now a tax calendar to monitor dates when there's a need to file various local and state tax reports as well as to review payments made? "

" Our accounts and finance people do maintain a tax calendar to monitor dates. They not only make sure of the taxes on the payments done, but also keep a report of it. That will be sent to you in detail to your email. "

" Does the firm use insurance service to protect its assets against possible risks? "

" Presently we take insurance services from Welda Insurance Corporate. They do a marvellous job at it , spot on. "

" Does the organization use honest and straight - forward marketing and promotion efforts? "

" We market our products & services through various search engines. And, you very well know that all the search engines review the ads before placing them in various websites. "

" Nice strategy of marketing! I'm glad I had an opportunity to audit your company. "

" I'm glad too. "

" So, that will be all. Thank you! "

" You are welcome. "

As soon as I was done with the work call I heard Jen in the back stand up on her feet, I had seen her walk into the room wearing nothing but her bath robe, her hair wet and glistening.

" Some trouble you got there? "

" Not at all, the numbers are huge so I asked him to send me a detailed email. Would you mind checking it for me tomorrow when I will be busy in the session? "

" Done "

" You are awfully nice today. Once a blue moon occurrence or when you really, desperately are in need of something "

" I can be nicely awful as well. do you want me to? " she said as she walked closer to me

" Don't be a pain Jen "

" What do you need Martin? You can come straight forward with the statement and say it. I know you want to "

" What I need is nothing, and what I very much want is your help this project on hand "

" Why did you call me here? You have not received the email yet, have you? Can't help you until you do "

" True "

" So what is it that you need, Martin? "

" Don't provoke me "

" Oh it's been done " Jen grabbed the collars of Martins satin blue button down shirt and kissed him passionately and ripped his shirt open

Martin lifted her up and kissed her down the neck sucking at places that will leave sordid and sinful marks for tomorrow

" Do you know how long I have been jerking off thinking about you? " whispered Jen " I need you so bad, fuck me. Make me come like you always do so well "

Mark grunted on her request and dropped her on the bed to penetrate and take her from behind, his mind wandered to Celine, shocked by the image of himself masturbating to her. He shook the filthy ideas that were invading his obscene mind and continued to make Jen scream out his name, banging her hands on the headboard.

" YES, YES, MARTIN, OH GOD YOU'RE SO BIG!! AH" she moaned and groaned aloud with Martin kissing down her neck and he increased the his pace.

- Celine –

On the way to the my daily run today evening I noticed Jen and Martin, sat way too close to be cordial friends. They expressions were of severe concentration, yet their hands seemed to be intertwined on the couch area between them. Martin was on the phone having a strictly serious conversation while Jen was sipping on her Red – bull and coke drink with her right hand busy with chastely typing down notes or whatever the hell it was she was engrossed into.

Seeing them together was always a hard - things, but I knew I had Martin in the palm of my hands when I needed him. His mind was solemnly devoted to his work, and heart to Jen or any other woman he might be with. But his eyes were always lingering, yearning for more and naughty in the sexiest way possible.

" Salut! "

" Celine! Hey babe! " greeted Jen, awfully happy to see me

" I hope I'm not disturbing you two "

" Not at all " she pointed towards Martin with her drink in hand almost spilling it on the floor.

" Can't speak for him though "

I looked over at Martin, his brows were furrowed and he seemed to be disturbed

" The accounts aren't balanced so I'll need you to send me proof, - No, no. Dick listen to me this is a- Yes, I know. I KNOW. Please don't let him touch my computer he- Yes. You'll receive them by tonight in your email. Alright, alright. Would you- OK "

" Eh looks rough! " I told Jen who was busy looking at Martin apologetically

" I know "

" He's such a dick! " Marin hung up his line and looked over at us and Jen simply shrugged at him. And he insisted on taking us out to lunch but Jen seemed a bit occupied and backed out.

" I will take a rain check on that offer, got a couple of things I need to care of. Sight – seeing still unchecked on my bucket list. "

" Would you like Celine to show us around? I know I would enjoy that! " Martin exclaimed

" Oh, I don't know if we have a free schedule today "

" Not today! Tomorrow? Or Friday sound good? " said Martin with Jen glaring at him with wide eyes and her mouth agape.

I could feel the tension and chose to take an easy road out of it but failed

" I have a job to get back at after, you know, the sessions here "

" We won't take much of your time, just a couple of hours? " This request came from Jen so I couldn't refuse. She seemed like a gentle hearted woman, looked tough but knew how to stay rigid and grounded. These past few days we have grown to know each other well and I couldn't possibly deny her request so I helplessly agreed to provide them with a quick and short tour around the Eiffel Tower and the Louvre.

- Martin -

Marta was the first one I noticed, everybody in the room had eyes for her. She stood 5 feet 11 inches tall, dressed in a pantsuit and sporting her red heels matching her similarly stained lips.

After the training I walked out towards the elevator when I turned around I noticed Marta was chasing me. Her woody cologne hit my nose as she tugged me inside the elevator and pressed the emergency stop button.

''I think I made it clear Marta, this isn't appropriate.''

''What is not?''

She started running her hand down my torso and grabbed my crotch massaging it. A loud sigh left my lips which she took as a consent and pushed her lips onto mine, tongues and everything.

''Damn it Marta! This cannot happen, so please stop and don't embarrass me'' I said pulling away from her and she was shocked

''I see the way you look at me Marten' she said with her thick and foreign Dutch accent.

''You can't fool me'' she hummed against my ear and she pressed the button to restart the elevator to exit on the 5th floor. Leaving a peck on my cheek and giving me last squeeze before leaving she said ''You know where to find me if you need a release" with a pout giving me a once over. Shit, I was so hard in my pants.

She was a smoking hot lady and there was no denying it. I could get in serious trouble messing with her. If only she was half as enthusiastic in our lecture and training projects as she was at luring me into sleeping with her. Sex with Ellis taught me the hard way to not mix business with pleasure, and the forbidden fruit is even more attractive and desirable when it's within your reach.

Especially if it's in a package like Marta's, who could get me hard in a single minute. I could run round the maze of berries but there is no place to hide anymore.

.............Chapter X I X

I went to my room to answer a call, looking at my phone I realised it was Ellis, speak of the devil...

" Hello "

" Hi, Martin " she said sounding a bit relaxed. Ellis and I spoke quite often. She has been to the city a couple of time to meet up with me. She even came by the office one time for work. Dick had called in a conference for over 50 employees to discuss a legitimate matter regarding an auditing inquest for various clients. Eventually, Ellis and I ended enthusiastically up in my apartment. The slow – going growth of our relationship was simply platonic, she had a boyfriend back home and I had my own commitments, which were non – existent; contrary to her purposely deceived perception.

" How is Paris? "

" Oh, it's nice. Eloquent "

" Ah Martin, you can anything but a man of short sentences. What is wrong? "

" Nothing is wrong "

" Martin "

" I think... " I said, unable to form a sensibly acceptable verbal explanation to what I was currently feelings

" I think I am being sexually harassed at work "

And the other end of the line blew up with raucous laughter,

" That was very helpful, Ellis "

" I'm sorry- oh god I'm so sorry. By who? I mean what happened? It's just you, alright I swear in the next 2 minutes I'll be a better friend. Tell me " she pulled herself together and cleared her throat

" It's just this assistant in my class "

" Is she good looking? "

" She's hot "

" And she harassed you? How? "

" She touches me and constantly persuades me into having sex with her, tell me to take my clothes off and "

Another boisterous laugh emerges from Ellis followed by her series of apologies

" I just don't understand why you wouldn't just sleep with her. Are you not attracted to her? "

" I don't know, maybe not. Maybe yes "

" Well you can always do the fore mentioned option, or just straight away threaten to expose her, get her disqualified from the programme which would cause a major hinder in her career so she will definitely be out of your hair "

" Yea, I guess. That would be so harsh though. Wouldn't it? "

" If she isn't behaving accordingly, there's consequences so, I would say no. It is not cruel at all, very essential to say "

I decided to withhold the incidents relating with Jen from spilling them to Ellis. It isn't like us to share everything and every little detail of our lives, but I think I was ashamed of it. Going back to my past isn't something I can be proud of and I had to take care of it. Although, I can't break things off with Jen over here while we are both stuck working together, I should certainly do it once we land back home.

67

. . . . .Chapter X X

- Jen -

" You should come down to the Netherlands someday, I'll show you around. It will be a fun, fun, fun thing to do yea? "

" Oh I'm not sure if my tight schedule will allow me to " Jen replied to Marta and her friend from the training session Juliana. She had awkwardly crossed paths with them when while being in the midst of scavenging down the coffee shops in Paris looking for a perfect blend of robust and Arabica coffee for her espresso shots. Jen wasn't one to befriend all the ladies at once but French/ European women seem to be rather neutral and easy going for her. She agreed to have some coffee and tarts with them and they got to talking

" That is too bad, I would love to have you there in my home " Marta slid her fingers on her knuckles and brushed them teasingly

Jen scoffed apprehensively feeling a tinge of nerves and was taken aback for a minute. It had been a long time since she had been intimate with a woman. She didn't mind making love to a person as long as she felt attracted to them, never based on their sexuality or gender. And Marta's beauty and appealing voice never went unnoticed which made Jen feel like she was desired. She glared up at Juliana who was now busy with her phone, her slim fingers fum bled with the screen typing too quickly.

" I will take that into careful consideration any time I am in Holland, thank you Marta "

" OH if you come down to Spain I could show you all around too, I have a beautiful olive garden, in my backyard and a fancy bungalow of my parents. We can rest up at beaches too, we have so many there "

" Thank you guys for the offer, I guess if you ever come to America I could show you around, touring at stuff " Jen hesitated as she offered with a tiny pinch of generosity. She did not want to hang out with these women for any longer. And –

" So Jen, what is your relationship like with Mr. Martin Muller? " Juliana perked up as she mentioned his name

" We work together at the firm "

" That is all? That's surely not what we have heard! " Marta spoke with a trace of coyness in her tone

" I see " Jen replied to them, who had their elbows up at the table and their faces resting between their palms like little puppies waiting for their treats.

" I think I will, Yea- I will head back now. I really need to work on the internal central unit for the venue. And a long day ahead of me "

" But it is only 5 P.M. Surely you must be done by now? At least finish your coffee no? " Marta had a glimmering shine in her eyes.

Jen quickly grabbed for of the coffee mug that was peacefully resting over its china saucer, a stain of lipstick marked the rim of it and she looked over at Marta in raw confusion. Jen rarely ever wore lipstick, and she wore the colour red as blood maybe once in her entire life

" Oh, my bad. I might have wanted to sneak a taste " Marta teased at her while her hand rubbed Jen's exposed skin under the table which made her shudder

" Let us go back to my room, hmm? "

" Uh . . I'm flattered Marta but I really need to get going " said Jen wiping her mouth off with the velvety purple napkin and she heard Marta sigh aloud.

" You don't like me? "

" You're lovely Marta, I'm not sure if we should let this get any further "

" But I want you, your body is so petite and sexy " Marta hissed at her neck inhaling sharply " and your scent is making me lose my mind. Sweet and spicy "

" Ok " Jen basically moaned into her ears and grabbed her by her arm and they both rushed towards her hotel room. Stumbling and giggles as that caffeine might have hit too hard on them. They heard Juliana snicker behind them as she yelled " Have fun girls, come back soon! "

<h1 style="text-align:center">. . . . . .Chapter X X I</h1>

- Jen's room 7: 30 P. M. -

Back in the room both the women were wrapped around each – other and had their hands all over the other's rapidly heating bodies. A buzz of phone alerted Jen, which was still in the back pocket of her red shorts. Marta smoothed her palm softly over her thighs and dig it under the leg of her shorts causing Jen to squirm in her lap.

'' Who's that? '' she asked

Jen grasped her phone out her pocket noticed a text message from Martin asking her to visit him in his room

'' Uh It's '' Jen mumbled with an uncertainty and Marta smiled up at her

'' Why don't we call him here? '' she said with hands landing on the small of Jen's back hugging her tightly and Jen raised her brows at her

'' Let's have some fun of our own '' she bit down Jen's neck and nibbled on her pulse point and Jen texted Martin with her left hand quickly which read '' Get to my room asap! '' her right arm was exploring the front of Marta's exposed breasts.

'' Ah Jen, you're so good with your hands '' they hummed into their heated kiss as the door knocked right after 2 minutes and Martin walked right in

" Jen you- " Martin looked up at the sultry scene ahead of him and felt feverish on the spot " what the hell is going on here? "

" Come on in stranger " Marta sat upright resting back on her palms digging in the white spread out bed and crossed her naked legs, she still had those red high heels tied on her manicured feet

" Jen? " Martin looked over the other side of the bed where Jen was sprawled and squinted her eyes at him

" What? Don't say you won't enjoy it. Shut the door please and get in here. If I don't come in another minute I'm going to be extremely frustrated " Jen scoffed and threw herself on the mattress with a hop

" We will take care of that for you " Marta sneered down at her and a coy smile formed on her lips as she reached down on the floor and wrapped Jen's legs over her shoulders

" Marteen a little help? " She turned her head to see him and smirked at his bulge peering out his tight jeans

" You could use some release as well " she remarked pointing at his pants and he obeyed to join in with them. He quickly undressed himself and stroke her hair as she spread Jen's legs wide open, sucking and licking into her.

The room's temperature shifted into a humid and scorching hot one, Martin climbed over the bed and Jen pulled him into her mouth, slurping and popping over his head.

The whole passed red hot as the three of them meticulously and pleasured each other, exploring every dishevelled and thirsty part of their clashing skins. It was a blur of Martin being laid on the bed with Marta sucking him off all the while jerking him with both her hands, and Jen who was sat on his face as he tongued her with each thrust ripping a snarly moan and grunt out of her as she tugged at his hair.

And another when both the ladies pushed him down, Marta giving him a wholesome taste of her as he sucked her raw until they came into the other's mouth in a 69 position, while Jen was on her knees nipping at his groin area and thighs giving a little help along causing two mouths and tongues teasing him.

They all lost count of how many times they came and ended up napping in the bed together, after ordering room service and watching crappy television.

" I didn't know you enjoyed being touched by women so much " Martin wore his bath robe and glanced at Jen who was busy serving herself from the food cart

" Don't act like you didn't fantasize about it " she said and threw a small piece of cheddar cheese at him

" It was amazing "

" Hmm tell me about it. I love Europe! " Jen grinned at him

Marta walked into the room after her shower which she insisted on Martin to join in, they might have ended up fucking against the shower door before heading out to eat.

" I'm famished! "

" Of course you are Marta. Here, you can have the whole tray " Jen was possibly in love with her now.

" Martin! Hands off! And get at your side of the bed, gosh you are so annoying! " Jen groaned and pushed at Martin who was sprawled about on bed like a star – fish.

" Let me sleep, I need the rest you both wore me out pretty heavily last night. "

" OH yea? As if you weren't enjoying yourself in that little action you got for yourself"

" Excuse m- " Martin was interrupted by a door swaying open and Marta walking into it again. The flashbacks of her gorgeous naked body and soft salty skin coated his tongue again " Marta? Forgotten something? "

" OH yes, I forgot this. My phone " She grabbed her phone over the bed – side oak – wood table and checked it.

" And forget this " She lent low on the bed until her lips reached Jen's lips and tugged her hair behind her ear for Martin's view. She watched him as she dragged her tongue out to lick Jen's peckish lips under her, and bite at it gently humming into the last firm kiss.

" Lovely girl " she whispered at Jen with her gaze still locked on Martin's troubled eyes. HE knew she got off on this sexual frustration he had to feel in her presence, she made it sure for him to be aware of it. She tried to induce that particular desire in him and somehow always succeeded without fail.

" She seems obsessed with you " Martin turned his attention towards Jen who seemed to be almost half asleep now as Marta headed out the door.

" Mmm. Jealous? " she asked him

He scoffed at her and changed the subject, " I have to say, you caught me off guard last night "

Jen's eyes fluttered as she smiled wide at him and blinked one eyes open her sleep deprived face shining up at him.

" Caught you off guard you say, how so? "

" Just didn't know you liked that sort of stuff "

" What sort of stuff are you talking about? Care to elaborate Muller? "

" I didn't know you liked sleeping with girls, or girls with men "

" You do know that I'm bisexual right? "

" What?! "

" Uh duh! I am. I mean I hooked up with Heather once. Oh boy were we hammered that night! "

Martin looked flushed as if the whole blood in his system was shot up to his head. He held the duvet over his bare chest and huffed a long breath. The mere idea of Jen with other women was fascinating to him. He could not possibly deny the sexual attraction that has been intricately grown into a grapevine of lust and likelihood.

" I did not know about that incident. Heather seemed so uptight so I wouldn't have guessed. When was it? "

" So you can visualise it? "

" Would that be so bad? "

" No. Whatever floats your boat. It was two years ago at the office Christmas party, she was so drunk she began whining about how she has a terrible choice in men, and how unlucky she is when it comes to choosing the right man. I was trying to hype her up and tell her she is a special lady who should not hang around people who fail to see that. She threw herself on me first chance she got and I liked it. You should have seen her face the next day, she seemed so embarrassed and puzzled. "

" Hmm, and how did you handle that? "

" I told her to take it easy, you won't know sexuality it's like a pool of various flavours you have got to try first until you land on the ones you are comfortable and familiar with. And I made sure she didn't feel any ounce of regret in her heart. "

" Interesting " Martin said with a perplexed face expression and got into deep thinking with his eyes narrowed on the ceiling above them.

His eyes studied the magnified Golden lining over the edges of the raised concrete which collectively formed a large star above their heads. It resembled a Satan's ritual ring as if the guests were invited into their den of crystals and fairy stones. The entire room seemed a mixture of neoclassical art and modern furniture along with the glazed glass window which displayed a pretty view of the whole city's skyline.

" Why the sudden urge of knowing about it all? What is the reason behind this unusual curiosity build up? "

" No reason. Just a little curious about it all. "

" Nothing to do with your own sexuality? Perhaps you want to explore the other gates and entrances, you know, get to know what you like or dislike? "

" What the hell are you suggesting? I'm not gay "

" Why are you acting so defensive. I will let you that there is nothing wrong with being gay, it's the 21st century for god's sake! Grow some balls Martin "

" Why would you make this about me? I was only asking you how your experiences went! "

" Forget it, I'll just... " Jen lined her lips with her forefinger and thumb pretending to zip her lips and tossed away the key in the mid – air "

" Alright you know what? You are free to think what you want to. It's not like I carry a board that says honourable personality on my back "

" Are you implying homosexuality as a dishonourable act? "

" I am just saying I don't carry a good name around here, which means that people have tons of rumours circulating around me "

" So, we have 3 more days to go "

" I know. it went too fast. The sessions were shockingly good, I hate to say I might have refreshed my own skills and techniques while teaching them with our peers "

" True, and I hate to say that our " peers " are actually pretty cool to be around. Especially the cruise day was a stand out for me "

" Oh yea. So apart from Marta who is your favourite? "

" Ukh Martin! Are we back on that pesky roller coaster again? "

" Come on, who would you have for our next time? "

" I thought you didn't want to keep doing this? Those are your words, letter by letter spoken by you "

" I didn't know any better. So what do you think about Celine? "

Martin rolled over and started smoothly running his fingers down Jen's exposed back. He felt her tense up under his grasp immediately regretting his choice of name favouritism

" You asked me about my obsession, tell me your s with this Celine chick "

" I thought you had a good thing for her too "

" I did, I do but not in that way "

" You don't think she is attractive? "

" Nope "

" I'm sorry are you blind?! " Martin shot right up and Jen followed him up and she grabbed her stuff to get dressed

" You know what, I think I'll just rest up in my own room. Nobody breathing down my neck or talking about who we should fuck next for his fantasy Greek orgy "

" This was your idea Jen! "

" This wasn't my idea! Marta was the one who called you in and I just went with it. And here you are naming more women to fuck around with. When will you ever stop Martin? I'm done with this "

And those hurtful words Jen stormed out of the room and Martin felt a ping of pain. He went to the bar that afternoon and drank away his stupendous worries.

Later that day Martin still felt restless and uneasy so he went out for a quick run. He wore large athletic Nike shorts which allegedly fell down his knees along with a white V neck top. He plugged his ear – phones and turned his playlist on his I – phone called " Blast Action ". IT was a mixture of Arctic Monkeys, AC / DC and Fleetwood Mac, rock was his style of getting into fast action. He felt his legs burn with each hit across the hard concrete and felt like he saw someone familiar in his peripheral view.

" Hello " said the meek voice from behind him as he took his plugs off and turned around to face Celine.

She wore body hugging bicycle shorts with a crop tank top, the blush in her cheeks and plump lips matched perfectly with the hue of her athletic outfit.

" Hey there! So you are a runner then? "

" Yes " Celine nonchalantly replied to his inquest and headed to run faster yet he decided to not lose path and keep levelling with her speed.

" The weather seems perfect for a short relay "

" Why are you always muttering rubbish about the weather? "

" I notice the good things in life? " He replied with a hint of a doubt in his rather unsure statement.

" Good things? " Celine started to sound out of breath as she struggled with her words and her chest heaved with sharp inhales between her sentences " Nature? Weather? And Women? "

Martin breathed out a loud guffawed laughter while shaking his head sideways, " You can say that "

" You know, you never really told me about what you had heard earlier "

" Pardon? "

" About Jen and I, what you've heard about us from your " gossip sources " " Martin's fingers did a small air quotation at the last two words and his eyes locked on the glowing sparks in Celine's gaze.

A cunning smirk took place on Celine's hot face and her eye lids were heavy with exhaustion smeared over her tired features. Yet. All that ran in rapid circles inside Martin's head was how hot she looked. Even when she was not supposed to, even in an overly – sweaty and irked condition she managed to look better than half the women he had slept with through - out his active life,

" I didn't take you for a runner, a gorgeous one at that " he complimented her with hopes of winning her over slightly adding a touch of spark between them.

" I didn't take you for a frisky runner after a long drinking session "

She motioned her thumb as a bottle dropping it down her mouth. The gesture caused another breathy laughter out of Martin. At this point he was not aware if he truly found her hilarious or he was smitten to the point of ignorance and blind idolisation.

" Mid – day drinking habits are more harmful than you would presume Mr. Muller "

" Why can't you just call me by my first name? Just Martin for you. M a r t i n " Martin air dropped the letters while pausing in his step as soon as he felt a jolt in Celine's step as she abruptly stopped running and began to hop mercilessly on her fast feet.

" I am on first name basis with people who I'm friends with. We aren't even on the level of acquaintance " She jogged on her bouncy neon orange Adidas Ultra – boost pair of shoes as she spoke to him

" We can be friends. You should know I can be very nice and supportive. I have many, many long lists of great friendly traits "

" I'm sure you do "

" What are your hobbies? Maybe we could spend sometime this week we can get together and do that. "

" We're merely work mates. Two people who work together in a professional setting. Just because we came on a " on the spot training trip " doesn't make it all of a holiday for people to bond "

" People who work together can be friends. There's no rule book against that. " Martin argued back almost immediately

" Why are you so persistent on the specifically befriending me? "

" Because I like you "

" You like me? " A high pitched note arose in Celine's voice

" Yea I like you. As a person, as a friend, as a co – worker... I think we can be co – workers without making it over the top. Contrary to what you might think, I actually enjoy talking to you as well. That's there, you have it. I am a pretty straight forward person ''

'' A man with a motive. I like that '' Celine's eyes dragged notoriously over Martin's entire body from his lousy shoes to his roughly gelled hair. She grinned at him with her drooped eyes crinkled on the sides.

'' See you around, Muller ''

'' Wha- oh you're such a tease. Such a tease! So You are just going to lose the Mister from my name? That's neat. Real neat! '' Martin scoffed at Celine who ran with ahead giving him one last turn and a little wave with her dancing fingers. There is definitely something going on between the amidst all the stress, Martin was glad to have another woman to chase. He knew the boring life that was waiting for him back home and simply wanted to blow some steam off and have fun. Especially at the end of his trip he really was adamant on spending his time wisely, and by wisely he meant girls, booze and the young long nights of Paris. He was not sure had gotten into him that day, it could have been the 10 rounds of gin and tonic he had carelessly thrown back at the Hotel bar.

. . . . .Chapter XXIV

" I must admit that it was super difficult to decide what, in my opinion, would be the must-see things in Paris that a first time visitor should cover – there's just so much to see, do and eat in Paris! " Celine rushed around the corner of the Eiffel Tower

" Ca va tres bien, et toi? Merci beaucoup! " She kissed a friend goodbye who seemed to be a tourist guide and waved at him

" Did you two want to climb up? "

" I don't think so I'm pretty worn out as it is " Jen claimed from behind. She wore a floral sleeveless top paired with some jean shorts and Martin had suede tan trousers on under a clean knit blue sweater.

The birds chirruped as by walkers passed through them, it was pretty cold that day with a slightly warm sun shining meekly shining through the massive dark grey clouds.

They had ice cream cups, each one a different mix of flavours from fruity to easy caramel crunch. Celine chose a blend of dark chocolate and raspberry mousse which made Jen scrunch her nose at her taste.

" I'm a classic vanilla person "

" You look like it too, what about in bed? " Celine asked Martin

" Everything but Vanilla in there " Jen interrupted them both and slid to walk between them. Martin rolled his eyes on her immature behaviour since he despised jealous people. Besides, he thought he made it clear that they were only fooling around and nothing serious was to be held up against him. He had mentioned it to Jen who agreed with the solid terms set forth before they commenced any further.

They spent the entire afternoon wandering around the famous bridges and antique stores which caught Martin's attention. Stopped for brunch at the Local café by the tourist filled streets.

At 4 P.M. they took a cab down to the Louvre museum which was highly recommended. Celine briefed them throughout the street, pointing at basic tourist packed areas and avoiding the trafficked roads. She carefully guided the driver and seemed like an impressive guide for them.

" Among my favourite highlights are the Classical paintings, Ancient Rome collection and Napoleon III's Apartments. " Celine spoke back at Jen who was admiring a painting behind her. Tracing her eyes as if she was admiring the magnificent artwork of brave strokes and a blend of antique colouring.

At one point in the evening Celine and Martin were elsewhere while Jen was lost in the crowd. She dialled up Martin and asked him to hurry up. She wanted to purchase a few souvenirs for her friends back home, and didn't want to stay out too late. Before heading back to the hotel they drove down to the local gift shops with a variety of chains and show pieces of snow balls and dancing musical boxes.

" So how do you have a mix of British and French accent on your tongue? "

" I grew mostly in Hampstead, North of London with my father and came back here for my studies- "

Celine was rudely disrupted by his phone call and she frowned at him

" Sorry, it's Jen I have to take this "

After he got back from his call he apologised to her again

" Your girlfriend is very possessive of you, protective too "

" Girlfriend? If you're talking about Jen I'd like to clear it and out it out there. She's not my girlfriend "

" But she told me she is "

" She did? That's weird "

Martin made a mental note to have a serious talk with Jen when they got back. As much as he enjoyed fooling around with her it was not an inch closer to being in a real relationship. It wasn't acceptable of her to act ignorant and walk around spreading irrelevant lies to people. He knew for certain the repulsive act was to get back at him about earlier when he made an honest yet ignorant suggestion to her about getting a three – way with Celine.

After our momentous trip and their rather quiet ride back home, I walked back to my room in solitude. Neither one of them stopped me to ask me to join them in the hotel bar – side for a drink they spoke to share in the car.

" I will order the drink you had on our day out " said Martin

" You would love that, don't pull my leg Martin! " giggled Celine in her sweater paws.

Her fierce demeanour and sharp tongue fades as you get closer to get to know her, she is a lovely woman. She looked like a woman who promises you the mighty heaven and rainbows in a silver platter with tiny emeralds of her colourful and earthy personality, and actually delivers it without any fail.

I undressed myself my thoughts still lingering on Martin's body, his hard pecs and swift abs twitching with each touch of my tongue on his smooth skin smeared itself as an unobscured image in my head. With my eyes closed and mind practicing sinful flashbacks of the best experiences I had sexually had with him, I laid back in the tub which bubbled with lavender and lukewarm bubbles that perfectly enveloped my hot body.

I began to sway my body feeling the warmth of the water diffuse all my tensions away, and the lucid images in my head made me even more hotter than I felt, so I turned the tap on with my right foot. I slid my palms down my chest all the way to my torso, gently squeezing my nipples which made me squirm.

I rubbed my right hand, gripping at the skin between my inner thighs and moaned out his name absent – minded, I dropped my head back letting the crispness of the water and salt mix away and indulge.

When I was close to reaching my hand down the aching spot, I heard a loud notification ring that brought me back to attention. Another one ringed louder than the previous one so I headed back in the room to check my phone, hoping it would be Martin asking if he could come over. Though that wouldn't be such a Martin act to be polite about his visceral needs, and I was correct. It was Dick, "such a turn off "

" We need to come back effective immediately, Charles has found a way to improve and upgrade our technical equipment and is in dire need of your assistance. "

" The plane tickets have been emailed to you, see you soon. "

..............Chapter X X V I

- Jen -

I packed my stuff by evening last night so I would not have to face the unfortunate chances of being late or missing my flight. If in any of the cases I accidentally were to miss my flight. I am sure the firm would not compensate for my ticket and ask me to rip my very tight and light purse strings to pay for my own plane ticket fares back home. I took some extra samples which were scattered about in the Hotel's bathroom and lobby carts and stuffed them carefully in my carry – on purse.

A knock on the door caught my attention and I ran up to see who it was, although I knew it was Martin.

" So you are really leaving? "

" Looks like it yea "

" He could not let you stay just for another day? We are leaving in a day. You could have gone back with me "

" You know I don't stand a chance against his requests "

" This firm is a hell hole I swear. "

Martin scratched at his neck from behind and stepped in my room looking a bit distressed. I decided to take that sadness and display of discomfort as his hurtful feelings due to my departure.

" You will be alright with – out me "

" I know. Who said I wouldn't be? "

" You just seem a bit troubled. That is all "

" Oh, right. I was thinking of shifting actually, you are the only person I have mentioned this to now so please don't go around spreading news "

" What? What do you mean by " shifting " And when have I ever been the rumour train captain? Don't talk to me like that "

" Oh? Who was the one going round telling people about us being in a serous relationship and spreading false rumours? "

" Wasn't me "

I was busted for my coy actions and I didn't want for him to know any of those things. It was a huge mistake on my part one wild night when I got so drunk off my face that I told everyone Martin and I were a serious couple. It was the envy built up inside of me that got the worst out of me in the spur of the moment. I felt my face turn hot red with a flush of embarrassment which I am sure he noticed because now he came to stand in front of me.

" Jen, don't lie to me. I can see right through you now. Why would you do such an immature thing? "

" Am I going to stand here and listen to you throw trashy words at me? Nope "

I turned around to reach out for the door knob but Martin held me in place with his firm grip.

" I don't like you telling people lies about me, you can say all you want about yourself but don't drag my name with it. You get me? "

" What have you turned yourself into Martin? Look at you! Let go of me! "

" I am so, so very cheerful that you are leaving me alone here. I don't ever wish to see you again " Martin grit his teeth with each hurtful word that came out of his mouth. His hold on me grew stronger and he pushed me against the door. A rush of tears escaped my eyes and I felt the burn under my face robust and explode.

He felt a shock of realisation hit him when the words that came out of his mouth were heard by him. He instantly let me slip out of his gripping hands and switched to walk backwards.

" I- I'm sorry I didn't mean that. Jen – "

" You know all I ever wanted was for you to feel the same way I did! I never ever behaved selfishly like you did! " I couldn't control the outburst of painful sobs and honest words that slipped out of me

" I- I wanted for us to work so bad that I tried to behave differently thinking that it was the way to keep you on your toes. I NEVER thought it would only end up driving you away from me Martin. Never! Every time I see you looking at women like Celine or – or Marta, how do you I would feel Martin? Remember the party where I thought we slept together and oyu told me we didn't? I was so hurt that day but I did not show it. I have the decency to act accordingly and cover up my personal emotions when it comes to working with you. I went as far as finding new jobs and failed because I knew I would not stand being so distant and away from you. "

" Jen I am so sorry. I didn- why didn't you tell me everything? "

" You think I knew it? I didn't know about my feeling until it hit me that day. When I got jealous at the sight of you licking Marta open, fucking her on my bed! "

" It wasn't my idea, you can't hold me accountable for that!
"

" Well it was not my idea either! Marta was so hooked up on getting in bed with you, I saw how her eyes watched every single move you made in class. She tried her best to gain your attention and being the cunning bitch that she is. She used me to get to you! How do you think that makes me feel? Huh? "

" This is all too much for me Jen. "

" I didn't expect any more from you. Have a good life Martin "

" Jen, don't leave like this. I came here to drive you to the airport not have a fight with you. Let us solve this like two grown adults "

" I am sorry that I said that about us being together but in my defence I was drunk, and high. "

I waited for Martin to say something on his end but it was silence that accommodated the room.

" I don't think there is anything more left to be said. I think I should just- I am leaving. "

" Jen, wait " I heard his voice husky and tired behind me and halted in my reluctantly slow paced steps

" I can't tell you I feel the same way, I never will. What we have is great but I cannot go beyond that. I love you but it's platonic "

" Great "

" I don't want us to fight anymore. None of this would have happened if you were acted sensibly and told me how you really felt. I would have never tried to hurt you intentionally, and you know how much I care about you "

" Do you Martin? Do you really? "

I folded my arms as a sign of neglect and asked him again,

" Do you care about me at all? "

" After all these months if you really choose to conclude it with the assumption that I do not care you " He paused for a minute to think and I prayed to god he would say something I hoped for. But –

" If you really do then there's nothing left to say. I can't do anything to change your mind it's all in your head "

" Thank you, Martin. Really thanks "

" Jen- "

" Thank you for being such a repulsive ass - hole! "

I left the room with my stuff and hand bag dangling loosely over my shoulders and ran towards the elevator. A helpful assistant rushed into my path and helped me by carrying my carry – on purse and laptop bag which I insisted on keeping " I got it thanks, you can take care of my suitcase, it is pretty heavy. Thanks "

He handed me some tissues after noticing the wetness under my eyes and nose and I grabbed it while thanking him one last time.

Martin messed with the last straw and I had nothing left to give him anymore. I needed to go back to work and change departments. I could try to steer away from him, tell Human Resources to never pair me with him on any future projects. What hurt me the most is feeling futile and the sharp ting of worthlessness.

- Martin -

After Jen's sudden departure and the best threesome of my life, I had very little left to do here. A couple of more sessions for a single last day were remaining with the Auditing assistants. And I had my mind fixed on finding a job in Celine's firm. Even though it plausibly won't work out I had to keep my options wide. I wonder how Dick would react if I mentioned my brewing idea of moving companies with him, I don't suppose he would be very happy about it. When I think of all the factors and reality of the blunt change in my routine it, sort of, hits like a wrecked train and throws me off track.

I have a final dinner planned with Celine tonight and it's going to be amazing. She is a great personality and time just flies by when I'm with her. The last time we hung out and drank out guts out at the bar we came back to our hotel rooms after sunrise. Some would take her as an uptight French woman, but she was a contrasting person in reality when you get to know her. I have had re – occurring thoughts about her naked body in my mind and jacked off to her pictures in my room alone. She also mentioned to me about her many colourful lovers all over the world, she travelled a lot on the job with her level of linguistics and interpretation skills. I bet a million dollars that she is an animal between sheets and would love to get her in bed. It doesn't seem like she would mind it, but I need her to make the first move.

I've had plenty more action this past week than I had the entire summer. It blows my mind how hesitant I was to arrive here for work, yet it turned out to be one of the best decisions made by me. I love Paris, the city of love, sex and sweet booze.

- Celine -

I could always sense a sexual tension between me and Martin, even in the presence of his lover. He seemed to be calm in his attire and very attractive when engrossed in his work. Our dinner was interrupted with the entire staff joining in with us on the table. So we had very little alone time and tomorrow morning was his flight back to America so I needed to make a move. Capre diem, no?

'' Where is Jen the tech gal? '' One of the auditing staff on the table inquired as she pulled her chair closer to the table.

'' She had to leave early for work back at the firm '' Martin replied to her after a questionable amount of seconds passed by

'' Do you miss her? '' I whispered in his ear for only us being the only ones able to hear my words

'' No, I don't. We are just co – workers with a little bit of history. But that is all it is. Just history ''

'' Alright, it is what you say it is. ''

'' So you will finally believe my words over the obnoxious rumours you heard? ''

'' I will believe what I want to believe, Martin ''

'' My name sounds so classy coming out of your mouth ''

'' Does it? ''

'' Say it again ''

" Martin " I enunciated on the 't' and 'n' while it rolled out of my tongue like honey. His cocky smile grew wider and he slightly tilted his head in my direction

" Lovely "

" Martin, this whole week felt like vacation with you! The work came on smoothly and we learnt so much. Honestly I don't think any of us regret coming her or getting to experience working with you " Josh from technical department spoke out. He was the one who chose to replace Jen for a single and last day of the auditing training session.

THe entire table agreed in unison.

" And the Cruise trip was a great catch too, it was so lovely! Thank you Marin. You're a good egg! "

Marin smiled at ol' Jean and frowned at her comment of weird terminology his American mind might have failed to perceive correctly.

" It's a saying. It means you are a good man, both feet on the ground and down to earth individual "

" Sounds well enough "

" It was a compliment " I sipped on my drink as I reminded him to be modestly respectful towards Jean.

" OH, thank you Jean. And everybody. This entire week would not have workout out as strictly smoothly it turned out to be, if it wasn't for you constant support and morale ethics. I'm truly honoured to have met you all "

" To a week in Paris " Martin held out hnis glass of glossy champagne and cheered to the table. Everybody else joined him and a hooted " cheers " came from all around the table.

Everybody were snugged comfortably in their respectful hotel rooms when I snuck out of mine. I wore nothing under my coat, and left very little to his imagination. With sharp motives and a barely cognitive mind I went to his room. I knocked twice waiting for him to answer the door staring at the blank white wooden door. After a whole minute passed by I sighed in my own defeat and went back towards the elevator but the door sprung open.

" Hi "

" Bonsoir "

" Celine! Hi! What – uh what are you doing here now? " Martin asked with a hint of playfulness in his dark eyes. His smile suggested that he knew why I was knocking on his door past midnight. I had a wrench coat on and nothing underneath which is probably the first thing he noticed.

" I reckon there is something with me that you need " I walked into the room and gently shoved him back as I entered. Placing the end of my belt's strap in his hand I backed to the door, which made the coat swing open. I threw the coat off my shoulders and faced Martin who was already shirtless in his position leaning on the wall. His muscles flexed with each step he took towards me and I felt the heat run down my spine.

- Martin –

I had to stretch my body first thing this morning, I was awfully tired and exhausted by my night of 3 hrs sleep. Just how I had pictured it, Celine was inclusively daring and incredible in bed. We had done a round 4 until she finally decided to head back to her room to sleep.

A bouquet of peonies caught my attention with a little card that read, " It was fun while it lasted, wish you a good life. Celine xx "

The thought of going back to the conventionally boring routine was a bit distressing bur heading home sounded appealing. Even though, the fear of having to face Jen still lingered in my mind, I had to purposely get skeletons buried in my closet.

My bags were packed and all the essential paperwork was signed off. A load of work was eagerly waiting for me and I could mentally prepare myself on the plane ride, send a couple of emails to arrange a proper plan set.

I got ready for the day heading into the office to greet everybody good – bye. Marta was already at the table watching me eagle – eyed. She slid me her contact card in the inner pocket of my bomber jacket. Her lipstick stain marked on it.

" It was lovely working with you all, and my pleasure to share my knowledge with the amazing crowd we have here. Wish you all a wonderful and successful life ahead. Martin out! " I gave my final speech and was over – whelmed by the excessive and unexpected love I had received from the team here. Having hugged and high – fived a couple of people I left the conference room with the happiest grin on my face. IT was then I noticed Celine who was standing next to the doorway which leaded towards the exit.

" I thought I could drive you to the airport"

" You really don't have to. I'm sure you have a busy day and it's too early. You should get some rest or did I not tire you out last night? "

" Hmm, you did a pretty good job at that "

" I wouldn't call it pretty "

" No? " Celine smiled at me with her blue eyes crinkling under the warm sun, she walked towards her navy blue BMW and unlocked it open.

" Come on in, I know a great café we can pass by for breakfast "

" Eh don't think I can eat now "

" Paris Charles de Gaulle Airport it is. Hop in "

Also get book #1:

A Martin Muller Audit #1

TOO DEEP
IN WITH
THE
AUDITOR

Whoever thinks auditing is boring
doesn't know what happens
between the numbers.

A STEAMY ROMANCE
BY MARINA PETERS

Don't miss out!

Visit the website below and you can sign up to receive emails whenever Marina Peters publishes a new book. There's no charge and no obligation.

https://books2read.com/r/B-A-XFPL-SEROC

BOOKS 2 READ

Connecting independent readers to independent writers.

Did you love *Auditing and French Kisses: Whoever Thinks Auditing is Boring Doesn't Know What Happens Between the Numbers.*? Then you should read *Un Caliente Crucero Steampunk*[1] by Marina Peters!

[2]

Bajo el caliente sol brasileño, esperando como la última de la cola para embarcar en el crucero a Nueva York, Monica Jackson, no está para nada encantada. Asignada como auditora a este crucero temático de Steampunk, el viaje va a ser más trabajo que diversión. Pero entonces otro pasajero está haciendo cola detrás de ella. Y cuando una voz profunda y aterciopelada de atrás le desea un "Bom dia" se da la vuelta.

---

1. https://books2read.com/u/b6KpQx

2. https://books2read.com/u/b6KpQx

Al ver al hombre alto, fuerte y guapo, comienza a esperar un crucero más prometedor y caluroso de lo que jamás podría haber soñado.

Read more at https://marinapetersbooks.com.

Also by Marina Peters

Martin Muller Audit
Auditing and French Kisses: Whoever Thinks Auditing is Boring Doesn't Know What Happens Between the Numbers.

Standalone
How to Generate and Earn Royalty Income
A Steamy Steampunk Cruise
Rare Gemstones and Unknown Precious Stones
Un Caliente Crucero Steampunk
Une Croisière Steampunk Chaude
Generating eBook Income for Intellectuals: A Comprehensive Guide to Creating and Monetizing Digital Books

Watch for more at https://marinapetersbooks.com.

About the Author

Marina is a part-time Audit Director working for one of the big auditing companies. She likes her job, all the beautiful things in life and writing. She loves her husband and her two kids. As writing is Marina's passion she combines all the topics where she has expert knowledge with writing. Thereof grew some non-fiction books and also the fictional Martin Muller Audit series.

Read more at https://marinapetersbooks.com.

www.ingramcontent.com/pod-product-compliance
Lightning Source LLC
Chambersburg PA
CBHW031335160726
47993CB00002B/688